# OF COBBLERS AND KINGS

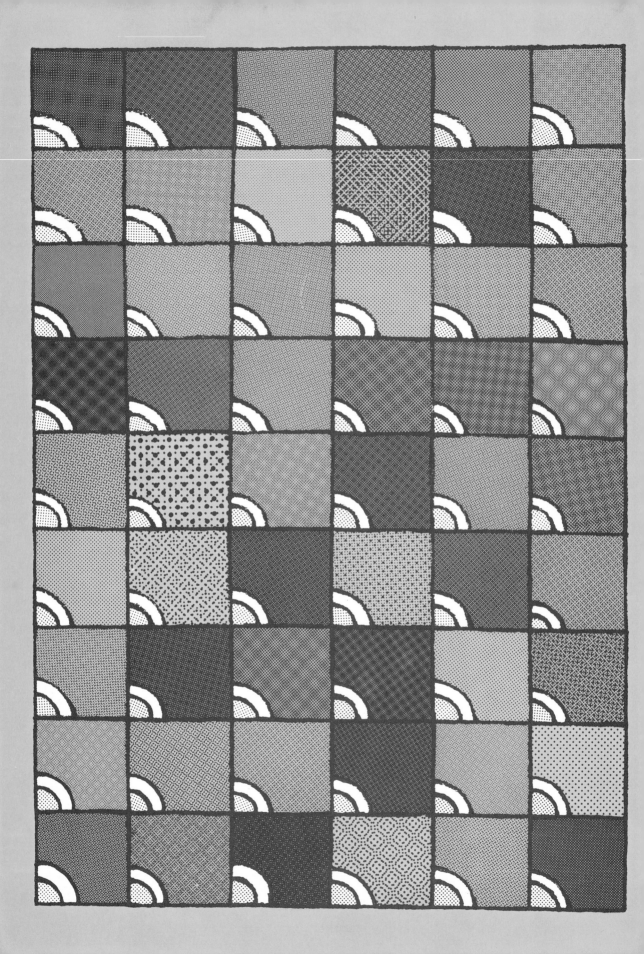

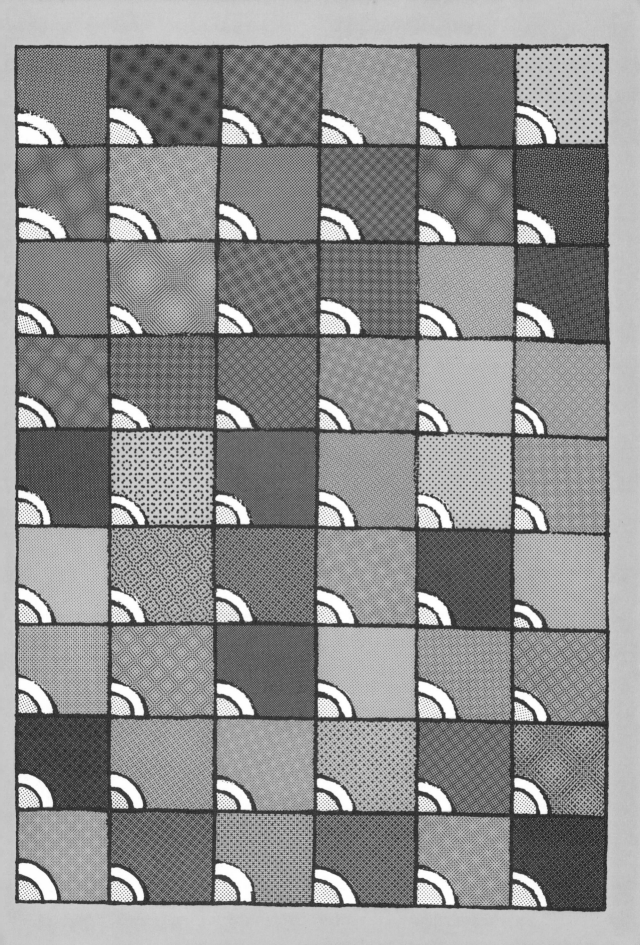

# OF COBBLERS AND KINGS
## BY AURE SHELDON
## PICTURES BY DON LEAKE

Pippin Paperbacks

PARENTS' MAGAZINE PRESS/NEW YORK

*For Stuart*
              *A.S.*

*To Reynold Ruffins and Simms Taback*
                          *D.L.*

Text copyright © 1978 by Aure Sheldon
Illustrations copyright © 1978 by Donald R. Leake
All rights reserved. Library of Congress catalog card number: 77-24725
Printed in the United States of America
A Pippin Paperback published by Parents' Magazine Press
10  9  8  7  6  5  4  3  2  1
*Of Cobblers and Kings* is published in a hardcover edition by
Parents' Magazine Press, 52 Vanderbilt Avenue, New York, N.Y. 10017
ISBN 0-8193-0927-3

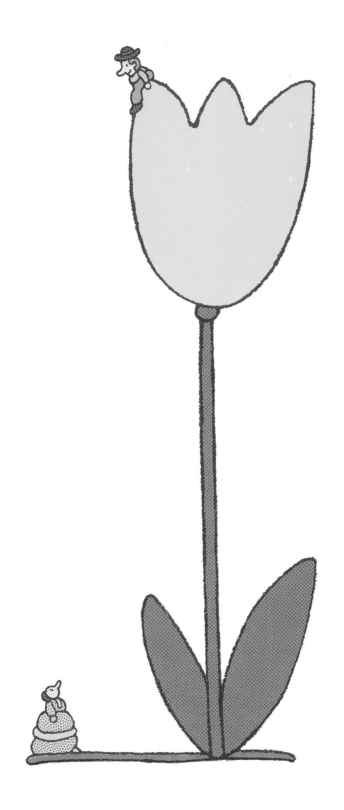

Once upon a time, in the far off kingdom of Shodd, there lived a clever cobbler named Gallo. The merry tap-tap-tapping of his hammer could be heard from sunup to sundown. He was Shodd's only cobbler, and a good one at that.

Now it happened that a carpenter came one morning to fix a fence across the road from Gallo's shop. This workman took one nail after another out of his apron pocket, looked at it closely, then tossed it impatiently over his shoulder. "My good fellow," asked Gallo, "why are you throwing away all those nails?"

The carpenter looked puzzled. "Would you believe that every one has its point at the wrong end?"
Gallo examined the nails carefully, then laughed. "No, no," he said. "These nails are simply meant for the other side of the fence."
"Of course!" cried the delighted carpenter. "Why didn't I think of that myself?"

When the townspeople heard how easily Gallo had solved the carpenter's problem, they all said, "Anyone so smart deserves to be Mayor of this town." And they insisted that the cobbler take the job.

A little sadly, Gallo hung up his cobbler's tools and locked the door of his shop. "I'm not sure I will like being Mayor," he thought. "But I shall do my best."

As Mayor, Gallo arrived at the Town Hall each morning just in time to see the caretaker shinnying up the rainspout and disappearing into an upstairs window. "I'm much too old to be climbing about like this," he grumbled to Gallo one day. "Then why don't you use the door?" asked Gallo.
The man sighed. "I keep forgetting my key."

After considering the matter carefully, Gallo hurried off to his old neighborhood. In no time at all, he returned with the carpenter, who sawed a second doorway right beside the first. But the new entrance had no door at all! Never again would the caretaker have to remember his key.

Everyone cheered and said, "Gallo can do anything! We must have him for Governor of this province."
Gallo wasn't sure. "I have no idea how to be Governor," he said quietly. "But I shall try my best."

As Governor, Gallo strolled to the State House each morning just as the clock in its tower was striking six. All day long he signed stacks of papers, gave speeches, made promises and cut countless ribbons on important occasions. Gallo seldom sat still, yet his work never seemed to be done.

The bakers, the housewives, the children, the farmers and even the bankers of Shodd were having the same trouble, though each one scurried about from sunup to sundown. "Something is wrong," everyone complained. "There just isn't time enough in the day to finish our work."

Again, Gallo thought carefully. And again, he hurried back to his old neighborhood. This time he went into the clock-maker's shop, where a symphony of clinkings and plinkings could soon be heard. After a while, Gallo left the shop with a mysterious bundle under his arm.

A curious crowd followed him back to the State House and watched in astonishment as their Governor climbed the tower. Gallo carefully removed the old clock. In its place he put a new one with sixteen hours on its face instead of the usual twelve!

"Now we shall all have more time to finish our work," he announced proudly. "Let's get busy."

The grateful citizens agreed that no one was smarter than Gallo. "Surely he must become Prime Minister of all Shodd," they declared.

"Oh, I could never be Prime Minister," protested Gallo. But the people would not listen. At last he consented. "I can try," he sighed.

Gallo was lonely in the grand house that went with the Prime Minister's job. It seemed that all he ever did was go to meetings at the King's palace next door.

Now it happened that the King of Shodd was fussy about his clothes, and it annoyed him greatly when the bottom of his favorite robe became ragged and dirty. Unless something could be done about it, the King refused to march in the People's Day parade, an old and popular celebration in Shodd.

The royal cleaners scrubbed and brushed and mended for at least a month. But the robe looked no better for their pains. At last they turned to Gallo for help.

Gallo looked the robe over carefully. Then, dashing back once more to his old neighborhood, he knocked at the tailor's door. Gallo asked to borrow his biggest and sharpest pair of scissors. As the Prime Minister cut, the tailor sewed a generous hem. In less time than it takes to tell, Gallo ran back to the palace with the King's favorite robe.

The King was overjoyed. He marched proudly in the People's Day parade, Gallo by his side.
"Long live the King!" the people cried. "And long live Gallo, our new Grand Chancellor!"

"Never!" exclaimed Gallo. "I cannot be Grand Chancellor." But before he knew it, Gallo was living inside the palace itself, doing all the things a Grand Chancellor must do. He spent his mornings making wise rules and his afternoons counting the royal treasure. Now and then he pinned a medal on a hero. But mostly he felt a little useless and more than a little sad.

Whenever Gallo rode through the streets of the kingdom, people gathered along the way to cheer. Even little children craned their necks to catch a glimpse of the Grand Chancellor.

On one such ride, Gallo noticed that the children were all barefoot. Some of the grownups were, too.

"Stop this carriage at once!" he cried.

Gallo stepped out and called a little girl to his side.

"Where are your shoes, my child?" he asked.

Curtsying, she replied, "I have no shoes, Excellency."
The other barefoot children answered in the same way.
"Can this be true!" exclaimed Gallo. "Our children have no shoes?"
"Begging your pardon, sir," one father said. "But we have had no cobbler in Shodd for some time."

Gallo returned to the palace in silence. He went to bed without his supper but did not sleep. He was thinking more carefully than he ever had before. Suddenly his mind was made up. In the stillness of the night, he crept out of the castle.

Long before the sun was up, the door to Gallo's cobbler shop stood open once again. The dust and the cobwebs had been swept away, and from within came the merry tap-tap-tapping of a hammer.

Old neighbors were amazed to see Gallo back. He was smiling and whistling a catchy tune as he turned out one pair of shoes after another.

"But...but..." stammered one neighbor.

"What, what?" laughed Gallo.

"But you are Grand Chancellor," another finished grandly.

Gallo kept right on with his work. "Of what use is a Grand Chancellor," he asked, "when all Shodd's children are barefoot?"

He finished sewing on a buckle. "What Shodd really needs is a cobbler," Gallo said with a wink. "And I am clever enough to know that is the best job for me."

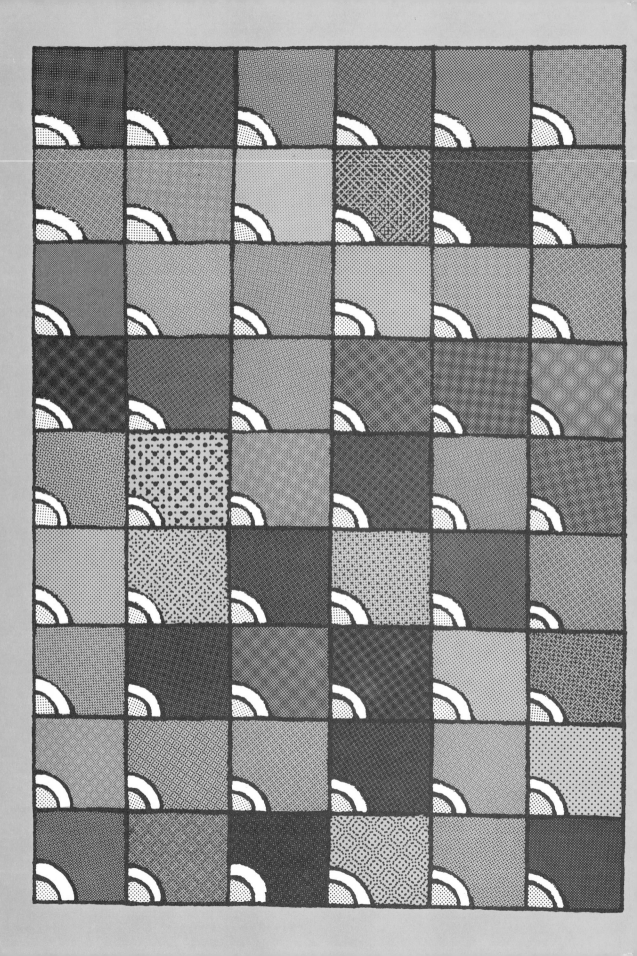

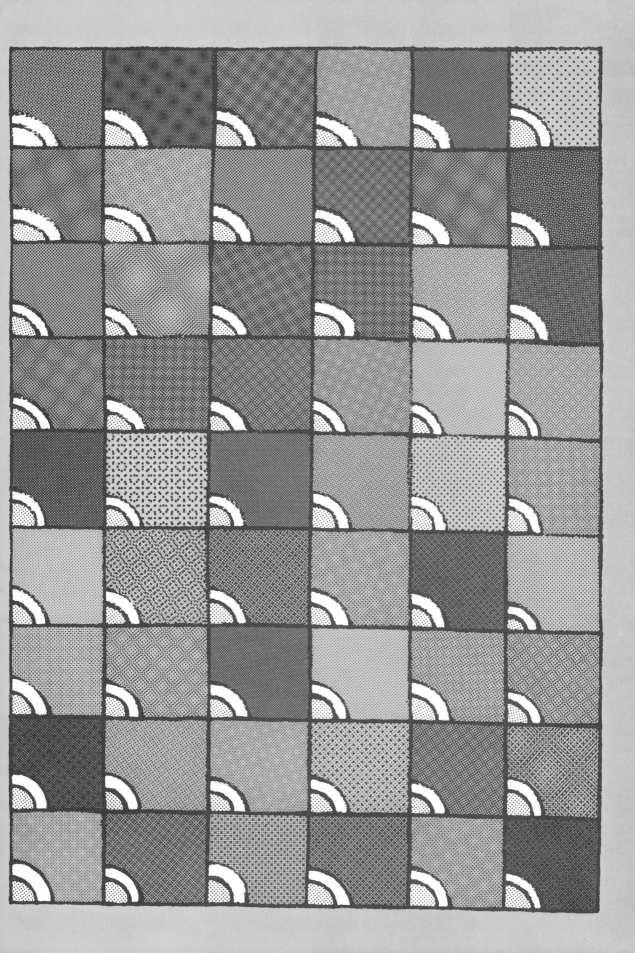